Mr. Belvedere's Rocket Candy Shop

Edited by Willie Grady

Cover Art by Phillip Perozo

ISBN 978-0-9913155-05

Printed in the USA

First printing 2016

Book design by Robert Lee Harris Jr.

Harris-Payne and Walker

Contents

Houston

Far and away in a dark galaxy, a radio operator signals his colleague to initiate the launch sequence for a rocket.

"Affirmative Houston!" the Captain answers. "Initiating rocket launch in, 10... 9... 8..." The Captain flickered the controls to prepare the rocket for its mission home. The rocket began to ignite, and the engine howled like a werewolf gazing into the moon.

All engines are running!" the Captain affirmed. He grasped the controls and guided the shuttle towards its destination. But suddenly, an unidentified object headed towards the rocket, striking the crew inside.

"Houston, we have a problem!" the Captain warned. The rocket started to experience immediate engine failure, and the radio communications went silent.

Lollyfudge

Suddenly a book fell to the ground causing an awkward silence to fill the air. The golden brown hands of an old man grew weak as he read to his grandson about space.

"Grandpa Pilot, are you ok?" Wisely asked. Pilot took a deep breath and wiped the sweat from his forehead with a handkerchief from his coat pocket.

"Yes!" he answered, "I'm just getting old." The two sat in an old rocking chair laughing and looking into each other's eyes as they watch the beautiful night sky.

"Grandpa, are the moons' made of candy?" Wisely asked, scratching his head. The moons' glowed brightly like a flashlight in a dark room and were more colorful than a box of brightly colored marbles.

"That's some imagination you have there!" he answered with a slight chuckle, "but yes it is!" Pilot put his arm back around his grandson and smiled.

"Do aliens live in space?" Wisely asked. "What about Zombies?" Pilot again laughed and raised his tired old hand to the sky.

"You see that shooting star?" he asked. "That is a magic rocket landing on the moon."

"So you're telling me that zombies ARE

real?" Wisely asked. "I didn't know zombies ate candy." He continued as he asked his grandfather a barrage of questions. "Have you ever been inside a rocket? Have you ever met an alien? What's the moon like?" The old Pilot leaned over from his chair and grabbed the book that had fallen between his feet.

"Long ago, I was the kid who saved the world." an old and tired Pilot said, "and it's all here in this book." Pilot opened the book and read aloud. "It all began fifty summers ago..."

Pilot & the 50 Summers'

It all began fifty summers ago at the Blue's residence. There lived a boy named Pilot Blue and his courageous puppy Rip. The two had an inseparable love for each other that could not compare to other kids and their puppy. Together, Pilot and Rip were a courageous pair who often loved to go on adventures. They were also big fans of Cowboys and Indians; as such they often got lost in their imaginations while playing. Pilot and Rip grew up on 1016 Lollyfudge Circle; chasing away pirates and other creatures that crossed their path as the day turned to night. Their missions always took place in the backyard; protecting their neighborhood from monsters and bad guys. Lollyfudge was their home, and the two had every inch of it secured.

Pilot had golden olive skin that complimented his red shirt and a brown fighter jacket that he'd forever wear. He had light brown eyes and black hair that gently touched the back of his neck, making him a heartthrob. Pilot's teeth were bleach white and straight as a ruler. He spoke with a raspy yet courageous voice and never feared a challenge. Wearing a pair of Chuck Taylors,' Pilot was fast as lightning and could jump higher than the moons' could float. Pilot was a hero like no other and stood ready to prove his worthiness to any challenge. Together, as a team Pilot and Rip could conquer the world.

Rip was Pilot's best friend and companion. He was a stuffed animal made in China and sent to Mr. Belvedere's Candy Carnival Circus long ago. Rip had pointed ears like a wolf, and he closely resembled a German Shepard in many ways except for the color of his fur. His bark was scratchy, and his fur was dark gray and tangled. The dark fur was immersing and covered his entire body except for a light gray patch that appeared on his chest. His nose was pink, and his eyes glowed green like an apple. None of Rip's distinctive qualities stood out nearly as much as the silver dog tags hanging from the bright red collar around his neck.

It was a usual day in Lollyfudge until everything changed for Pilot and Rip. They would again, have to put their friendship to the test in the adventures of Mr. Belvederes Rocket Candy Shop.

The Emperor of Sweets

Every day, Mrs. Blue took Pilot to school, but today was different. The leaves of autumn fell swiftly through the air as Mrs. Blue buckled Pilot into the backseat of the car.

"Get em' Rip!" Piloted shouted.

"Roof... Roof!" Rip barked in a scratchy voice. He barked at a jellybean that lay on the back seat next to Pilot.

"The Jellybean Beetle works for Mr. Belvedere!" Pilot yelled in a raspy voice. Trumpets began to play loudly as he and Rip were again lost in their imagination and headed to battle with the rotten candies that surrounded them. Pilot nor Rip was afraid, and would never accept defeat at the hands of a few pieces of candy.

"Pilot... Pilot... are you listening to me, Pilot?" Mrs. Blue asked. Mrs. Blue turned and tapped Pilot on his shoe.

"Yes, mommy!" Pilot answered. Pilot often got lost in his imagination as the world changed before his eyes. No adults saw the imaginative world that Pilot could see nor bothered. He glared into the world fully alert where anything could happen.

It was a Friday and Gully Shoots birthday. She was turning eight today. She was Pilot's sweetheart and a great friend. Everyone was sweetheart and a great friend. Everyone was later expected to gather at Pilot's house to celebrate her birthday. Mrs. Blue arrived at Mr. Belvedere's Rocket Candy Shop to pick up one order of purple-gecko cake before she took Pilot to school and then headed to work.

"Mom, where are we?" Pilot asked. Pilot held Rip firmly as they looked at the massive building.

"We're at, Mr. Belvedere's Rocket Candy Shop!" His mother responded. Pilot's eyes grew wide as he talked to Rip.

"We need to be careful!" he whispered. Pilot and Rip had no idea what awaited them inside and were anxious to find out. Every kid in Lollyfudge dreamt of standing where Pilot and Rip stood, and the two were almost inside. Rip sat on Pilot's shoulder, and the two stared in awe at Mr. Belvedere's mysterious candy shop.

"Are you ready?" Pilot asked. Rip shook his head and grinned at Pilot. The doors to Mr. Belvedere's Rocket Candy Shop slowly opened, and the two followed Mrs. Blue into the store.

Mr. Belvedere's Rocket Candy Shop was filled from top to bottom with sweets and chocolate that filled row after row; and treats that glittered of every color in the rainbow. The air smelled of freshly baked cupcakes, brownies, and cookie dough. Mr. Belvedere owned every size, every flavor, and every type of candy ever made and created more with each passing minute.

"It's as we dreamt it to be!" Pilot said wide-eyed, looking at Rip. The two became filled with hunger just from being around the many delicious snacks and treats that their bellies desperately wanted to eat.

"Let's get some candy!" Pilot suggested. Rip jumped from Pilot's shoulder onto a shelf filled with tacky taffy and golden butterscotch candy.

"Good boy!" He applauded. Rip grabbed a couple of pieces and quickly jumped back onto Pilot's shoulder; holding the candy in his mouth. They chowed down on the tacky taffy and the golden butterscotch candy as they walked around the store with Mrs. Blue.

"Pilot... did you take some candy?" Mrs. Blue asked.

"No mommy... !" Pilot answered with a mouth full of candy, "I didn't."

"Well... don't touch anything!" Mrs. Blue fussed. She glared and pointed her finger at Pilot, to let him know she was serious.

"I won't!" Pilot answered with his fingers

crossed behind his back. Pilot gave his mother the best puppy face a kid could give.

Suddenly the air became cold, and the room got dark. Pilot and Rip's teeth began to chatter as they chewed on the tacky taffy and golden butterscotch. Behind a set of mysterious doors came the sounds of vicious monsters and beasts that echoed throughout the store.

"Rip, what do think it is?" Pilot asked.

"Roof. Roof!" Rip barked. Neither rip nor Pilot had any ideas about what might lie behind the doors ahead.

The doors slowly opened, and a creepy man entered the room, sweeping and dusting the floor, with his brown and yellow broom. It was Mr. Belvedere, an old man with big, thick, coke bottle glasses that made his eyes appear very tiny. Mr. Belvedere had puffy orange hair and was bald down the middle. He wore a white lab coat stained with colors never seen before. It was filthy from all the candy he'd make in the back, presumably behind those swinging mysterious doors. Mr. Belvedere hated children plenty, and with a passion, and so did his helper Sasha.

Sasha was a fat, long-haired, gray and white cat, with a pink nose. She was Mr. Belvedere's cat, and always went wherever he'd go. Sasha always ate snacks and hated dogs very much.

"Dogs, dogs, dogs... I hate dogs!" Sasha meowed the moment she saw Rip.

"Master, let me at him at once; I will crush him!" Sasha purred. "Meow... hiccup, hiccup, meow!" Sasha began to spit hairballs everywhere.

"Not now, Sasha!" Mr. Belvedere whispered. Mr. Belvedere began to pet Sasha's thick kitty fur with an evil, atrocious smirk.

"Hello, Mrs. Blue." Mr. Belvedere said in a slithery voice. "How may I help you?"

"I am here to pick up Gully's birthday cake." Mrs. Blue explained.

"One moment, Mrs. Blue," Mr. Belvedere replied. "Please wait here, while I get Gully's birthday cake for you." Mr. Belvedere left the room with an evil smile and a slightly menacing laugh as he entered the mysterious laboratory doors.

Meanwhile, Pilot and Rip dazzled around at the different candies in the store as the two still suspected something wasn't right. Suddenly, a light shined from a shelf filled with candy; drawing Rip and Pilot's attention to it.

"I wonder what that is?" Pilot asked. He and Rip slowly moved towards the light that shined

Rip slowly moved towards the light that shined bright like a man wielding iron.

"It's a rocket, Rip!" Pilot shouted. "It's a rocket." Pilot and Rip momentarily lay in wonder at the rocket's beauty.

"Rip, see if you can reach it." Pilot said. Pilot believed with the rocket he could save Lollyfudge from Mr. Belvedere and his army of rotten candies.

The moons were made from old candies long ago, and they were the only sweet candy left in the galaxy. In Lollyfudge, candy was no longer good nor sweet, but evil and rotten, and the children could no longer enjoy them thanks to Mr. Belvedere. He infected and spoiled all the candy on the planet and needed to destroy the moons to obtain total authority over the world's candy. Pilot had heard of the rocket in rumors but never knew it existed. The rumor was that the Rocket possessed magical powers. If ever a pilot who was highly noble and favorable presented himself along with a friend, of which true friendship existed, the rocket would explain the existence of Lollfudians', and save the planet from the chaos that the looney Mr. Belvedere had created. Pilot was going to stop Mr. Belvedere no matter what dangers lurked ahead, and all he needed was that rocket.

"We have to get our hands on that rocket!" Pilot shouted. "See if you can reach it." Rip pounced onto the shelf from Pilot's shoulder, trying to get his paws on the rocket. He climbed the shelves one after another, going towards the rocket as fast as he could. However, a few shelves ahead lurked an army of Muscle Gumballs; armed and ready to protect the rocket at all costs.

The Muscle Gumballs had mean eyes and the strength of ten lions within their shell. Their eyes were large, and their noses were black and shaped like a heart. They had long skinny legs and huge muscles that could tear children apart. However, that didn't scare Pilot or Rip, because they knew the Muscle Gumballs were soft on the inside and filled with delicious, gooey candy.

Jack Gumball Russell was the gumballs' infamous leader, an old cowboy and the last of a dying breed. He stood sternly in front of them like an unwavering block of steel, looking as strong as an ox.

"You'll never get this rocket," Gumball Jack yelled. "Attempting to do so will most assuredly end in failure!" The muscle gumballs began parachuting off the shelves towards Rip, like rain parachuting off the shelves towards Rip, like rain drops falling from the sky, and continued to do so by the dozens. Pilot tossed Rip a shield that was pinned to his fighter jacket to use against the gumballs. Rip caught the armor in his mouth and began to fight the gumballs one by one, dodging and blocking each attack. The shelves began to fall, and gumballs and candy fell from each wall. Rip started to become covered in gumballs and Pilot became worried.

"Are you ok, boy?" Pilot asked.

"Rurrrr!" Rip whined. Stars floated above Rip's head as Pilot helped him up.

"Time to go, Pilot!" Mrs. Blue said putting her receipt away. Pilot carried Rip in his arms and left the store with his mother.

"We'll get the rocket!" Pilot assured.

"Who are you talking to?" Mrs. Blue asked. She didn't understand why Pilot caused all the commotion.

"My best pal in the world, Rip!" Pilot answered. Mrs. Blue buckled Pilot into the backseat of her car and drove him to school. She stopped in front of Lollyfudge Elementary and smiled at the two.

Lollyfudge Elementary

It was ten minutes to eight, and Mrs. Blue was running extremely late. She arrived at Lollyfudge Elementary and needed to get Pilot inside quickly.

"Hurry up; mommy is late for work!" Mrs. Blue said. Pilot hated school and did not want to go inside. He'd rather be home sleeping next to Rip, watching cartoons.

"I don't want to!" Pilot whined. He tried his best to convince his mother to let him stay home.

"Nice try!" Mrs. Blue answered. "Now, go inside!" Pilot grabbed his backpack and jumped out the backseat of his mother's car. The two walked to the front doors of the school with a sad look on their faces.

"I really... hate school!" Pilot complained. "Especially Lollyfudge Elementary!" Rip felt Pilot's pain and licked him on the face.

"It'll be ok!" Pilot assured. The two entered the school looking everywhere for their friends but had no luck. After a while, the two decided to split up.

"I'll go left, and you go right!" Pilot suggested. Rip nodded at Pilot and took off running down the hallway.

The school was packed, and the chaos was

everywhere with no end in sight. Pilot and Rip continued to search everywhere for their friends.

"Roof. Roof!" Rip found a girl who looked like Gully and barked to get Pilot's attention.

"What ya got there, boy? Find somebody?" Pilot asked. Rip pulled on the leg of Tanya Taffy; the richest girl in Lollyfudge. Ms. Taffy was what you would consider a pure breed. She was also a born and raised spoiled brat and jerk, who didn't like Pilot, not one bit.

"Rip, let her go!" Pilot demanded. Pilot pulled Rip away from Tanya and apologized to her.

"Learn to control your mutt!" Tanya Taffy screamed. She slammed her locker shut and walked away complaining about Pilot and Rip.

"What's her problem?" Pilot asked. He did not understand Tanya's hostility towards him and Rip.

"Do you have a moment?" a familiar voice asked. It was Abraham Licorice who was running for class President. Lollyfudge Elementary was currently holding student government elections, and Mr. Licorice seemed to be a shoe-in as the next class, President.

"What is it?" Pilot asked.

"Four Score, and Seven Years ago!" Abraham Licorice answered. Pilot listen to Mr. Licorice for the next thirty minutes while he campaigned for the presidency. He and Rip anxiously waited for him to finish, and soon fell asleep with their eyes open.

"...And that is why you should elect me as the 16th President of Lollyfudge Elementary!" Mr. Licorice said. He gave it his best and convinced Pilot to vote for him.

"Have you seen, O'bey? Pilot asked. He could not wait to share the news of the rocket.

"O'bey is near the root beer machine if I'm not mistaken, and I saw your friend Gully already in class." Mr. Licorice answered. Pilot thanked Abraham Licorice and headed towards the juice
machine looking for his friend.

O'bey Capricorn was Pilot's mate, his best bud. He was a seven-year-old boy, who carried a toy guitar and wore a purple cape around his neck. His eyes were turquoise blue like the Caribbean sea, his hair was medium blonde and straight, almost like strings of gold. O'bey was from California so he also always had a pair of black shades on him no matter what the season or the weather. He talked with a distinct surfer accent and clearly loved music very much.

"O'bey the PF!" Pilot shouted. He and O'bey were pals forever.

"Pilot Blue; my people!" O'bey yelled. "What's going on amigo?" He put two-quarters into the drink machine next to his classroom. He pressed the button for the root beer, but nothing came out.

"Stupid machine took my money, dude." O'bey cried. "Not cool bro." O'bey raised his leg high in the air to give the machine a good whooping.

"I'll show you, who's boss!" O'bey threatened. He kicked the machine as hard as possible, but still no root beer fell out.

"Ugh, why do you treat me like this dude?" O'bey asked the machine. "Dude, I thought we were the best of friends!" Suddenly two drinks fell from the machine, and O'bey was relieved. He turned and looked at his pal, Pilot. "My most excellent companion!" O'bey said. He could see something was on Pilot's mind, so he eagerly waited for him to spill the beans on whatever news he had.

"I found the rocket!" Pilot revealed.

"The rocket?" asked O'bey.

"THE rocket!" said Pilot.

"Whoa! Don't lie to me mi amigo!" O'bey answered. O'bey had heard many rumors about the rocket and the magical powers it possessed. It was something he had wanted for quite some time.

The first period was about to start, and the two were going to be late.

"Are you ready to go to class?" O'bey asked.

"Yeah, let's go before the bell rings." Pilot suggested. "You know how Mrs. Honeyshoe can be." Mrs. Honeyshoe was the known to be the strictest teacher at Lollyfudge.

"Who are you telling?" O'bey responded. "She gave me a D on the exam!" O'bey handed Pilot a root beer, and the two hurriedly walked to Mrs. Honeyshoe's class together.

The bell sounded as Pilot and O'bey took their seats. Mrs. Honeyshoe was out with the candy flu and wouldn't be back for a few weeks.

"A substitute!" O'bey yelled. "Today will be a piece of cake." O'bey relaxed his hands behind his head, and his feet on his desk. He then talked to Pilot about his longtime crush.

"Pilot, there's your future wife!" O'bey teased.

"Talk to her, dude!" Pilot sometimes acted shy around Gully and needed to be pushed.

Gully had long, beautiful brown hair, and a distinctive cute laugh that everyone adored; not to mention the most amazing smile ever. Her eyes were hazel with blue and green spots, and her skin was olive tone. She was taller than most kids her age but very slim. She was the smartest girl in all of Lollyfudge elementary. Nobody else even came close to her smarts.

"Like, seriously!" O'bey asserted, "Talk to her!"

"Okay. Okay!" Pilot responded. He and Rip walked to where Gully sat and took a seat next to her. She was studying for Mrs. Honeyshoe's history exam.

"Martin Luther Candy Jr. was a candy rights activist!"" Gully read aloud. History and Science were her two favorite subjects.

"Happy Birthday!" Pilot said.

"Thanks!" Gully replied. Pilot twiddled his thumbs and lowered his head. He was always shy around girls but especially shy around her. It was difficult for him to look Gully even in the face.

"I thought you and O'bey were skipping class again today when I didn't see you!" Gully said. Pilot and O'bey were always skipping class, and Gully figured today wouldn't be any different.

"I'm trying to be good." Pilot replied. There was silence for a moment, and then Pilot leaned towards Gully and looked deeply into her eyes.

"What is it?" Gully asked. Pilot cleared his throat and spoke.

"Well uh...." "Well..... Rip and I found the rocket!" he said.

"Oh really? Where is it?" Gully asked. However, O'bey interrupted the two before Pilot could say another word.

"So what's going on with you two love birds?" O'bey asked. He loved to annoy Gully and often teased her.

"Be quiet!" she replied. "Where's your girlfriend, Lemon?" O'bey blushed, curled his eyes in the opposite direction and had nothing else to say. He just silently grabbed his guitar and struck a chord.

"Want to hear some tunes, dudes?" O'bey stood ready to share his music and waited for the others' to respond.

"In a minute." Pilot answered. He wanted to discuss the rocket with the others, and the plan he had to retrieve it.

"No prob bro." O'bey responded, "So what's this tubular plan of yours?" Pilot composed a quick plan to recover the rocket and shared it with the others. Afterward, he rested on a desk in the back of the classroom and dreamt about the rocket.

To the glaciers we go

"Rocket's red glare... Bombs bursting in air..." Pilot orchestrated the Lollyfudge National Anthem and dreamt of leaving the planet.

"Rise and shine!" Gully whispered to Pilot.

"You were talking in your sleep." "It's time to go home!" Mrs. Blue waited for the children in front of the school. Pilot quickly grabbed Rip, and the three headed outside to meet her.

"I call shotgun, dudes!" O'bey yelled. He called dib's on the front seat before anyone had the chance, but was immediately interrupted by Pilot's mother.

"It's up to the birthday girl." Mrs. Blue intervened. O'bey fell to his knees and begged Gully for her permission.

"Please, amigo, please!" he begged.

"Fine," she answered. "I was going to sit by Pilot regardless." Pilot's face turned red like a bright apple. He was utterly speechless and in total shock.

"Really?" he asked. However, before Gully could respond, O'bey interrupted.

"Gully likes Blue... Gully likes Blue," he teased. "Ugh, dudes!" O'bey enjoyed picking on her, and it was completely harmless.

It was now four o'clock, and two hours remained until their mission. Mrs. Blue and the

Mrs. Blue and the children arrived at the house, and prepared for a night of games and partying.

"We don't have long!" Pilot explained. He and the others went over the mission and went upstairs to prepare to get the rocket.

"Write this down." Pilot suggested. Gully listened carefully with a pen and paper while he called the items out aloud. The three of them gathered everything they needed and waited for their mission to begin. They all walked around, laughing and singing tunes.

"O'bey, can you play some of your best tunes?" Pilot asked.

"Sure thing bro," he replied. O'bey found himself a microphone and began to sing aloud. "Mr. Belvederes... Rocket-Candy- Shop filled with ice-cream... gumballs... and lollypops..."

The adults were in the backyard having more fun than the children. Gully's cake sat on the table and read, "Happy Birthday Gully" in huge pink letters. It stood almost six feet tall, with purple frosting, and five layers of cake in all. She was in love with her cake, and couldn't wait to have a slice.

"May I have a slice?" Gully asked. Everyone gathered around to sing her, Happy Birthday.

Gully blew out her candles and had the first slice of cake.

"This is beautiful!" She shouted. Pilot and O'bey grabbed a slice for themselves, and they all munched on the Purple-Gecko Cake together.

Thirty minutes passed, and it was time for games. The kids gathered near a tree to play licorice on the rotten candy and hit a piñata with Mr. Belvedere's face on it. Gully was first to hit the piñata, and stood in front of the tree, blindfolded and ready to swing. Sweat drenched down her blindfold as she raised the bat high above her head and let the piñata have it one good time.

"Great hit Gully!" Her dad applauded. Candy exploded from the piñata and landed everywhere in the backyard, making it shine like the colors of the rainbow.

"Yes!" Pilot yelled. Gully kissed Pilot on the cheek and smiled at him. He blushed and twiddled his fingers; dazed and confused.

"What was that for?" he asked. However, before Gully could answer, O'bey again interrupted the two.

"Gully loves Blue, Gully loves Blue!" he teased. O'bey held his stomach and pretended to throw up his lunch. He pointed at Gully and laughed until his lungs almost came up. Pilot paid no attention to O'bey and grabbed a candy bar from the broken piñata.

"Go long!" Pilot yelled. He threw a candy bar high in the air and O'bey ran like water from a faucet. However, his throw was off, and the candy bar swirled out of control.

"It's going wide!" Pilot shouted. O'bey followed the candy bar carefully and watched it's every direction.

"Look out for that cooler!" Pilot screamed. However, it was too late; O'bey ran smack into a cooler filled with cold drink. Mr. Belvedere Soda exploded everywhere, and he got stuck inside the cooler.

"Are you ok?" Pilot asked. "Amazing catch by the way!"

"Thanks, bro!" O'bey replied rubbing his head. He felt the effects from the crash landing in the cooler and laid on the ground half conscious.

"That's what you get!" Gully joked. She never passed an opportunity to tease O'bey and enjoyed every second of it.

"You're a Hero!" Pilot suggested. O'bey raised his head high and looked at Pilot.

"I am?" he asked. O'bey lowered his head and closed his eyes."I'll take you to the rocket-candy shop... candy canes, and lollipops..." The adults celebrated and were having a good time dancing to the music that played on the radio. O'bey's head spun in circles from the fall, and he could no longer think straight.

"Ladies and Gentleman!" O'bey announced. "I can hear the most rad and bodacious tunes!" However, the ringing he heard was just from him falling on his head, and the tunes were actually from the music his folks were dancing to.

"He's totally lost his mind." Gully said, "What is he talking about?" She worried for O'bey and looked at Pilot with a concerned face.

"It's the Ice Cream Glaciers!" Pilot answered. O'bey and Gully were confused and scratched their heads.

"Are you sure you didn't fall on your head too?" Gully asked. However, he was right; the Ice Cream Glaciers were ahead.

The Ice Cream Glaciers

Pilot and the others stood speechless, looking deeply into the horizon of the Ice Cream Glaciers.

The Ice Cream Glaciers were a mystical land of vivid colors, where the air smelled of freshly baked cookies and candies. Inside were mountains made of ice cream, with scoop after scoop of falling flavors. Sugar snow covered the glaciers mile after mile with cherry-blue turquoise and watermelon-orange indigo lakes that filled an endless horizon of beauty. The three had never seen anything quite so beautiful or amazing before in their lives and could not wait to enjoy it.

"I'll catch you dudes in a few!" O'bey shouted. "Going to hit some waves, bro!" O'bey ran for the red-velvet coconut pond and dove in head first. He backstroked around, spouting out water from his mouth like a fountain. Pilot and Gully joined him in the pond, and the three played together. They ate and drank the pond dry until their bellies filled with food and their hearts with fun.

After about an hour of playing, it was time for the children to leave and find the rocket. The three exited the water and headed to an icy trail nearby. Mr. Belvedere was very observant, and he knew all about Pilot and his friends plan to steal the rocket. He watched them closely from a magic jaw-breaker inside his mysterious laboratory and sent forth an army of rotten candy to stop them.

"Sasha, come here immediately!" Mr. Belvedere shouted.

"Yes, your majesty!" Sasha purred. She laid on a shelf next to the Muscle Gumballs, giving herself a bath.

"I have a job for you." Mr. Belvedere explained. He wanted her to stop Pilot and the others from getting the rocket. Sasha meowed at Mr. Belvedere and left immediately for the Ice Cream Glaciers.

As the children made their way through acres and acres, sugar snow covered ground, and they became cold and tired.

"We've been wandering around randomly for hours, and we haven't seen anything of significance. Gully complained. Her face turned red as an apple, and her snot dripped down like a nasty green icicle as the cold pounded the children.

"Whoa, cool dude!" O'bey joked. "Snot pop!"

"Quiet!" Gully yelled. Pilot interrupted the two from bickering, and searched for a place to rest.

"How about over there?" he suggested. Pilot pointed to a huge tree that sat in the middle of nowhere. Its branches were twisted and covered in snow, and green, apples that glowed. The three sat underneath the tree and rested for a while.

"This is our best adventure yet!" Pilot said.

"Totally!" O'bey answered. O'bey lowered his head and struck a tune from his guitar.

"Parents be tripping. Clean the room. Grab the broom. Sit up straight. Don't be late. Clean the kitchen. Stop your..... fidgeting" he freestyled.

"It's not the best!" Gully criticized holding her stomach. Gully was starving and her stomach began to growl. Luckily, a giant apple fell from the tree and hit Gully on the forehead.

"Ouch! Stupid apple," Gully grumbled. Gully rubbed the caramel from her forehead and tightly gripped the green apple in her fist.

"You're just a dumb, rotten, apple!" she bickered. Gully bit the apple expecting it to be sour. However, the apple was juicy and the best she had ever tasted. The delicious green apples were topped with caramel and filled with gummy worms.

"You dudes have to try some of this green licorice grass!" O'bey screamed. O'bey pulled the licorice grass from around the tree and stuffed it into his mouth.

"It's the best grass I ever tasted, dudes!" he cried. O'bey wiped a tear from his eye and devoured the licorice grass that now surrounded him.

Several hours passed, and the three again became restless in their search for the rocket. Pilot talked about the rocket, and the others listened carefully.

"Mr. Belvedere will not hesitate to spoil what's left of the good candy." Pilot addressed. Both Gully and O'bey agreed, and the three left the apple tree.

After a while, Pilot and the others came across a sour pony drinking from a lake. They were in awe of all of its amazing colors and wanted to catch it for themselves.

"Someone hand me a shoelace?" Pilot asked. Gully gave Pilot a shoelace from her pocket and watched him closely as he lassoed the shoelace high above his head. Pilot let go of the shoelace, and it landed neatly around the neck of the sour pony. However, the sour pony became frightened and quickly ran away with

Pilot trailing behind like a rag doll.

Oh Buddy, Oh Pal

Gully, O'bey, and Rip were alone in the Ice Cream Glaciers and lost. They were also worried about Pilot; for he was still missing and nowhere to be found yet.

"I hope Pilot's ok, and not hurt too badly!" Gully said. "I miss him and wish that he was here to guide us!"

"I'm sure he's fine" O'bey suggested. Gully was concerned about Pilot's whereabouts and lost without him.

"Knowing Pilot, he's probably got the rocket by now!" O'bey suggested with a smile and a lot of confidence.

"What should we do?" Gully asked.

"Simple! Take it e-z bro. Getting worked up isn't going to help Pilot or us." Obey answered. He stood up tall and mighty and cleared his throat.

"Foremost, we should ask ourselves, what would Pilot do?" O'bey said. However, neither were exactly sure what Pilot would do, so they sat there pondering the question and thinking to themselves.

"Wait, I've got it!" O'bey explained. "I know what Pilot would do." Once again, O'bey stood up tall and mighty with his cape blowing in the air.

"He'd... he'd go find himself." O'bey stuttered. O'bey still doubted himself and had no idea how to find Pilot.

"You're right. We can't give up. We've got to find our captain!" Gully agreed. The two knew finding Pilot wouldn't be easy, but they knew it wasn't impossible, and they would all end up going after the rocket together in no time. However, Gully nor O'bey knew where to begin.

"So...Where do we start?" Gully asked.

"I have absolutely no idea" O'bey replied. All was quiet for several minutes while the two thought over a plan to save Pilot.

"I got it!" Gully shouted. "Bring it on in." Gully kneeled into the snow and began to draw a plan to save Pilot. However, after doubting herself, she erased her idea from the snow and just sat next to O'bey.

"Never mind. So how about you, O'bey" Gully asked. "Got anything yet?"

"Nothing." O'bey replied. Suddenly the ideas began to hit O'bey like water hit the ground when it rained. O'bey jumped around bragging that he had the answer to saving Pilot.

"So... what?" Gully asked.

"We should use that nose of Rip's to find Pilot!" O'bey suggested. O'bey wanted to use

Rip's nose and his keen sense of smell to pick up Pilot's unique scent.

"You're right. I like that idea O'bey," Gully said with a smile on her face. Gully was eager to rescue Pilot and couldn't stand the thought that he might be in danger out there.

"Rip, come here!" O'bey called. O'bey grabbed Rip and began speaking to him in puppy language. Rip jumped from O'bey's arms and began to search for Pilot.

After several minutes of searching through the snow, Rip came to a pause in the snow.

"Did you find him Rip?" O'bey asked.

"Roof, roof!" Rip barked. Rip scratched at something that lied buried deep beneath the snow.

"Good boy! We found him!" Gully cheered. Gully sat next to Rip and began to help him dig.

"I don't know. Are you sure about that?" O'bey asked. He was uncertain what lied beneath the snow and had a strange feeling about what Rip scratched at.

"Sure. What else could it be?" Gully answered. "He's gotta be under the snow." Gully wanted to see Pilot again and begged O'bey to help to make it go by faster. O'bey fell to his knees and helped dig a hole.

"Dude, something's moving under there...." O'bey mentioned.

"I feel it too." Gully calmly replied. "What do you think it is?"

"I haven't the slightest idea." O'bey answered. The two stood up and carefully peeked into the hole.

"You see anything?" Gully asked.

"Nothing at all." O'bey answered. The knocks grew louder and louder as O'bey and Gully listened attentively.

Suddenly, a hideous candy arose from beneath the snow. It was Pancho Vanilla, the hardest Mexican candy in Lollyfudge. Pancho was made from pure vanilla ice cream and coated with a hard orange shell. Pancho had wild green hair and a scruffy black beard. He carried a slingshot and spoke with a voice that children feared.

"What's the big idea?" Pancho asked. The vanilla monster pulled a slingshot from under his poncho and began to shoot jaw-breakers at the two.

"We should run!" Gully suggested as sweat ran down her cheek and drenched her shirt.

"Not a bad idea!" O'bey nervously replied. Gully tugged O'bey, and the three ran as fast as possible from the monster.

"We need to find a place to hide and soon!" O'bey insisted. The two ran from Pancho Vanilla while they improvised a quick plan.

"Here's the plan!" O'bey explained. "Go left, and Rip and I will take the right!"

"Works for me!" Gully replied. The three split up and went their own way. Pancho Vanilla chased the two and could not wait to eat. He wanted a full tummy before returning to sleep.

"We're cutting this a little too close!" O'bey said looking at Rip, "we gotta hide and now." The two dove between the butterscotch bushes and sweet grass and held each other tightly. They waited anxiously for the monster to give up looking for them.

Meanwhile, Gully took a hard left into the caramel apple trees trying to avoid the monster.

"When I catch you, I am definitely going to eat you!" Pancho Vanilla growled. Pancho shot two jaw-breakers at Gully with his slingshot.

"Oh no!" O'bey cried. "He's going to eat her!" He and Rip watched from afar as Pancho Vanilla reached out for Gully.

"Make a jump for that licorice vine!" O'bey yelled.

"Are you crazy?!" Gully asked. "I can't reach

"If you want to live, better try!" O'bey explained. Gully looked at the licorice vine, took a deep breath, and looked at it once more.

"I can do this!" Gully whispered to herself. She took a deep breath, closed her eyes tightly, and jumped for the licorice vine.

"Wow. Did you see that?" O'bey asked. "I didn't think she'd actually do it, dude." Gully caught the rope and dodged Pancho Vanilla by an inch.

"Now what?" Gully asked. She ran from the monster and towards O'bey and Rip.

"Whoa, whoa, whoa dudette. Don't come over here, man!" O'bey pleaded. However, she ignored O'bey and ran towards him anyway.

"For real?!" O'bey said, "Ugh. She's going to blow our cover!" Rip gave O'bey the strangest look ever.

Pancho Vanilla had Gully and O'bey cornered with nowhere to run. Gully leaned over and closed her eyes while O'bey sweated profusely.

"Any last words before I eat the two of you?" asked the monster.

"Yes!" A mysterious voice answered. "How would you like to be served, hot or cold?" From the trees came a rider armed with a bow and arrow. It was Pilot riding the sour pony towards Poncho Vanilla. Pilot gripped the bow tightly and aimed it at Pancho Vanilla.

"So, you want a candy standoff, is that it?" Pancho asked. Pancho Vanilla grabbed his slingshot and aimed it at Pilot. The two pointed their weapons at each other and waited for the other to fire.

"Catch!" O'bey yelled. He tossed Pilot a match from his pocket to light the arrows. Pilot lit two arrows and let them fly through the air; it illuminated the sky like fireworks on New Year's. The arrows pierced Pancho Vanilla, and he began to slowly melt into vanilla extract. Pancho could no longer harm children, and was hurt badly. Pilot kneeled beside him and looked boldly at the monster.

"It has been an honor, Mr. Pilot Blue," Pancho said in a tired voice. "However, I am done for." The two shared a special moment together, and Pilot grabbed the slingshot from Pancho Vanilla's soft hand.

"I will be evil no longer, I have satisfied my thirst and do not hunger." Pancho said. At that moment, the vanilla monster melted away. Pilot explained where he'd been and helped Gully and O'bey onto the sour pony. Sasha watched from a caramel apple tree with disappointment as Pilot, and the others moved further ahead. She knew Mr. Belvedere would not be happy with the news, especially the news about Pancho Vanilla melting away.

Dessert Heat

The three reached the desert, and the air became hot like Eskimos visiting the beach in the middle of the summer. Above was a sky of marshmallow clouds, and ahead laid an endless desert of cactus cakes and brown-sugar sand. After nothing but a barren desert, O'bey became dehydrated and was on the brink of passing out.

"Hey, you guys..." O'bey moaned. "I don't feel so well."

"What's wrong?" Pilot asked.

"I can't bear this heat anymore," O'bey complained. O'bey could no longer tolerate the heat and passed out.

"Is he dead?" Gully asked. "Well... he does look a little pale. Pilot and Gully turned around and looked at their buddy. O'bey lay unconscious and stretched over the sour ponies back.

The heat intensified by the second and Pilot and Gully continued to search for shade, but nothing except miles and miles of brown-sugar sand appeared.

"Look at him, I'm getting a little worried," Gully said. "He's not moving." Pilot grabbed O'bey's arm and raised it high in the air.

"If it falls, we have a problem." Pilot let go of

Obey's arm, and it instantly dropped to the sour ponies back. Surely O'bey was out cold.

Ahead appeared to be cottage made of tootsie logs. Tootsie Logs were candies used for buildings in the Valley of Sweets. The words, "Candy-Bar" were nailed to the outside of the cottage accompanied by a no trespassing sign. Pilot and Gully rode the sour pony to the Candy Bar and tied it to the front with a shoelace. O'bey momentarily regained consciousness and peaked at the Candy Bar, however, he again fainted, and the two carried O'bey inside.

Inside, sat Pancho Vanillas cousin, Cinnamon Red. Cinnamon Red was a hot-tempered cinnamon who did not like children. He was one of Mr. Belvedere's rotten candy bullies and looked for Pilot and the others.

"Hey, boss!" a cinnamon said to Red. "Isn't that Pilot Blue. Pilot and the others were ordering Mr. Belvedere Root Beers from a gumball waitress nearby. O'bey half awake, lingered on a stool at the candy bar.

"How many fingers do you see?" Pilot asked. O'bey slowly raised his head.

"Two fingers!" O'bey answered, "maybe three..." O'bey felt dizzy, but would be ok. He sat up and looked around the candy bar.

"Awesome!" O'bey said giving a thumbs up to the others and taking a sip from his root beer. "Just what I needed." He and the others chugged their root beers and headed for the exit.

Nearby, Gumball Jack played go fish and drank Mr. Belvedere Root Beer with Billy the Kisses and Sammy Spearmint. He also looked for Pilot and now laid eyes on him.

"Where do you think you're going?" Gumball Jack asked. Pilot took a deep breath and turned around to face him.

"After the Rocket!" Pilot answered. He and the others again headed for the exit, but this time was stopped by Cinnamon Red. He blamed Pilot for Pancho becoming vanilla extract and wanted revenge.

"What did you do to Vanilla?" Cinnamon Red asked. Red became hot and charged at Pilot, however, Pilot dodged Cinnamon and leaped onto a stage where the famous musician 50 cinnamon performed.

"It's getting hot in here!" Pilot said, trying to get away from Red. Pilot made sure to keep his distance from the angry cinnamon monster.

"I'll show you!" Cinnamon Red yelled from across the room. He threw a fireball at Pilot, but missed and hit Gumball Jack instead. Gumball Jack's shell cracked, and a piece of it fell to the ground causing total silence to fill the room.

"Which one of you cinnamon's is responsible?" Gumball Jack asked. However, nobody answered him, and the gumballs and cinnamons began to fight one another.

The Candy Bar became rowdy with fireballs and gumballs ricocheting throughout it. Pilot grabbed Jacks broken shell and used it to cover himself and the others as they crawled to the exit and left the candy bar. Once outside, he and the others wasted no time and untied the sour pony. They rode into the hot blazing dessert and were relieved to have avoided disaster.

Graham Cracker Pyramids

Pilot, O'bey, and Gully rode into the blazing desert heat looking for the rocket. They barely escaped with their lives and felt lucky to be safe. The Graham Cracker Pyramids were a just a couple of feet away, and the three rode the sour pony towards them.

"What are those?" Gully asked.

"Zombies!" O'bey yelled. Hordes of marshmallow mummies came from the Graham Cracker Pyramids ahead.

"I'm scared!" Gully whispered. Pilot lit a few arrows and roasted every marshmallow he possibly could.

"Quickly!" Pilot shouted, handing Pancho's slingshot to O'bey. He and O'bey fought the mummies as they made their way closer to the pyramids.

"We're almost there!" Pilot shouted. He and the others yelled loudly for someone to help them.

"Open... Sesame!" Gully commanded. She remembered what the wise Abraham Licorice had once told her. "It's easy as Open Sesame."

The doors to the pyramid began to slowly open, and a glorious light filled the children's hearts with a feeling of safety. Pilot and the others entered the pyramid on the sour pony and were now safe from the horrible monsters outside.

Inside, Pilot and the others were met by the Bubblegum Soldiers. They were bubblegum who were strong like buffalo and protected the princess. The Bubblegum Soldiers wore military jackets, and their hair was thick like caramel syrup. They carried clubs made from tootsie logs and were sometimes both good and rotten candies. Their leader, Lt. Berry Bubblegum met Pilot and the others at the entrance of the pyramid He took their sour pony to the stable and quickly sealed the door behind them. On the highest orders, Lt. Berry led Pilot and the others to see the Princess in her chambers.

Inside the Princesses chambers, golden honey bars and lemon candy diamonds filled the room. It sparkled like a rainbow on top of a lagoon. The Princess had a waterfall of sweets that filled her own personal swimming pool and a golden throne to go with it. She ruled the Valley of Sweets for Mr. Belvedere and kept the rotten candies in order.

"I never met a princess," O'bey said as he stroked his fingers across the pool. "I can't wait!" The doors opened, and the princess of the Graham Cracker Pyramids walked in. Pilot and the others couldn't believe their eyes and stared in awe at her.

"You're the Princess?" Pilot asked. It was their classmate Lemon Belvedere from Lollyfudge Elementary.

"That, I am!" the Princess responded. Princess Lemon had green eyes and red hair like her father, Mr. Belvedere. She was eight years old and ruled the pyramids with an iron fist.

"Don't be nervous." Gully joked. She poked O'bey with her elbow and teased him about Lemon.

"Whatever!" O'bey replied. O'bey grabbed Lemon's hand and gave it a kiss. He could not stop staring, but neither could the princess.

"Will you help us?" O'bey asked. He wanted the rocket with all his heart and needed her help.

"The rocket?" Princess Lemon asked. "I suppose so." The Princess really liked O'bey and wanted to help him find the rocket. She led him and the others out the back of the pyramid and past the marshmallow mummies.

"Go to the Black Licorice Jungle." the Princess insisted.

Black Licorice Jungle

"She'll be coming around the mountain when she comes!" O'bey sang at the top of his lungs, and couldn't get the Princess off his mind. He was in love with Lemon and talked about her while traveling to the Black Licorice Jungle.

"Isn't she awesome?" O'bey asked, "I think we're in love!" O'bey drooled on Gully's shoulder while he dreamed about the princess.

"Who's in love?" Gully asked.

"Dude, the Princess, and I!" O'bey replied. Gully gave O'bey the strangest look a person could ever give to another.

"I doubt that." Gully insisted. She and O'bey bickered at each other as they neared the Black Licorice Jungle.

Pilot and the others stared deep into the darkness of night. The trees blocked the moon, and the stars provided a little light. Snarls echoed, and rumbles shook the ground, for they were vicious roars and howling sounds.

"I'm scared, Pilot!" Gully whispered. She clinched Pilot's waist tightly and dug her face deep into his back. Pilot assured Gully everything would be okay and rode through the vile and treacherous jungle on the sour pony.

The Black Licorice Jungle had chocolate pudding swamps with glow in the dark gummy worms and frogs inside them. Nearby, were crocodile candy pits filled with hungry starving crocs, whose razor-sharp teeth always chomped. Yellow eyes followed the children's every move, and they were stuck in the middle of it all.

"Hiss, Hiss, Kiss." A mysterious voice uttered. Pilot and others looked around with a face of fear. For they could not see anything, but a hiss they could hear.

"What was that?" O'bey asked. O'bey bit his nails and looked around for the mysterious voice.

"I'm not sure?" Pilot responded. "We better keep it moving." he spurred the sour pony to move faster.

After several minutes of riding through the dark jungle, it appeared. It was the voice that constantly whispered in the children's ear. It was a Spooky Cane Snake that spoke to the three. His stripes shined bright, and his face they could now see.

Spooky Cane Snakes had evil green eyes and a striped body that resembled a candy cane. Their leader was Colonel Creole, and he was the sneakiest of all Mr. Belvedere's creations. He was a blue and green snake who wore a brown fedora hat and disliked children. Colonel Creole searched long and hard for Pilot and the others and now took them as his prisoners.

"Sergeant Snake..." Colonel Creole hissed, "Take these children away!" Sergeant Snake led the children to a pretzel prison where they could not escape. Creole left to tell Sasha about the children's capture and was to return soon.

"What now?" Gully asked. "We're trapped with nowhere to go!" She looked at Pilot and waited anxiously for a response.

"Don't you worry. I'll think of something!" Pilot assured as he looked for an exit. However, Pilot seemed to have no luck.

Thirty minutes had passed, and Creole Snake had not yet returned. Pilot still looked for an exit but hadn't yet found any.

"Dude, it sounds like the guard is getting some zzz's," O'bey said. "Maybe we can get his keys. Sergeant Snake fell asleep on the job, and the three went over a plan to get the keys from the table which he slept.

"Let's send Rip to grab the keys!" O'bey suggested. All looked at Rip with a significant amount of relief.

"Great idea!" Pilot responded. He slipped Rip

through a hole in the gate and Rip grabbed the keys with his mouth and ran back to Pilot.

"You saved our life!" Pilot said as he grabbed the keys from Rip. Pilot kissed and hugged Rip tightly and opened the door minutes before Sasha and Creole returned. Once again, the children escaped by a single hair on their heads.

"Nincompoop!" Sasha meowed. "Mr. Belvedere will have your stripes for this." Sasha was angry and sent the Spooky Cane Snakes after the children.

Meanwhile, Pilot and the others traveled through the chocolate pudding swamps and licorice vines trying to escape Creole's Army of spooky snakes. They could hear the snakes getting close and needed a place to hide.

"Let's hide in here." Pilot suggested as he and the others crammed into a butterscotch bush. The three kept quiet as possible hoping the Spooky Cane Snakes would pass by them. However, the snakes were on their trail like bloodhounds after a steak.

"I smell children." the Colonel hissed. He and his army began to circle the bushes where the children hid. With nowhere to go, Pilot and the others came out of hiding and faced the Colonel and his army of snakes.

"Can I eat one of them boss?" a snake soldier hissed. The soldier stood fast and awaited Creole's orders.

"I suppose so!" Creole snaked ridiculed. Creoles army of snakes laughed at the children as the Colonel wrapped himself around Gully and looked deeply into her eyes.

"This one!" the Colonel insisted. He moved to bite Gully's arm, but in the sky, what looked like two shooting stars, fell two arrows. The arrows landed next to Creole and stopped him dead in his scales.

"Who's behind this madness?" the Colonel asked. It was Jolly Licorice, the leader of the Licorice Indians.

The Licorice Indians had hypnotizing eyes and hair made of licorice vine candy. They were the lost tribe of Lollyfudge and the sweetest candy left other than the moons'. They roamed the Black Licorice Jungle fighting off bad candy and keeping order in the Valley of Sweets.

"My people do not wish to fight!" Jolly Licorice informed as he stares a Creole fiercely.

"You have not a choice!" the Colonel answered. The Spooky Cane Snakes attacked the Licorice Indians, and things got crazy. Spooky Cane Snakes squeezed the warriors until they almost burst, and the licorice Warriors tied the snakes into knots and things got worse.

Creole tightly held onto Gully and took her high above the trees.

"Let her go!" Pilot demanded. Pilot grabbed a licorice vine and swung towards Gully and Creole. He pulled an arrow from his back and fired a shot at the Colonel, but missed.

"Last chance, Creole." Pilot warned. "Let her go." Pilot stood fearlessly before Creole ready to strike at the first opportunity.

"Have it your way!" Pilot said as he began to release the arrow from his hand. However, before Pilot could let go, a voice yelled for the fighting to cease. It was Princess Lemon coming from the dark jungle with the Bubblegum Soldiers. She ordered Creole to free Gully and to return to base immediately.

"Yes, my Princess!" Creole Snake acknowledged. The Colonel bowed to the Princess, and he and the Spooky Cane Snakes left. The Licorice Indians put away their bows away and vanished into the Black Licorice Jungle before anyone noticed.

"FYI, I wasn't hiding!" O'bey insisted. The Princess laughed and held his hand.

"We haven't long!" the Princess informed.

"Mount up." Pilot and Gully jumped on a sour pony and followed the Princess and O'bey to Mr. Belvederes Rocket Candy Shop.

The Candy Rocket

Pilot and the others arrived at Mr. Belvedere's Rocket Candy Shop with the help of the Princess. They needed a way inside, and the princess knew exactly how.

"How do we get inside your highness?" O'bey asked. Lemon looked deeply into O'bey's eyes and grabbed his hand.

"This way!" the Princess answered. She led O'bey and the others through Sasha's cat hole to get inside Mr. Belvedere's store. Pilot and the others were finally inside and were loving every second of it.

"Dude!" O'bey proclaimed, "I never imagined it'll be like this." O'bey cried tears of joy and fell to his knees for having been in the presence of the Rocket. He always wanted to see the inside of the rocket shop, and there he kneeled before it.

"The Rockets in here." the Princess advised. Lemon knew where to find the rocket and led Pilot and the others directly to it. She pointed to the mysterious doors made from pure honey gold and precious stones that stood before them.

"Wow, it's beautiful!" Gully replied. She glanced at Pilot and took a sigh of relief. She, like O'bey, had never been inside Mr.

Belvedere's store and enjoyed every second of it.

"O'bey, watch this!" the Princess said. Lemon walked to the gate and whispered an ancient Lollyfudge riddle that unlocked the mysterious doors. She and the others wasted no time and quickly entered the dark room.

Inside Mr. Belvedere's workshop was dark like a house at night with no electricity, and the air froze like water in the winter. Pilot and the others could not see anything and needed to find the lights.

"Where's the lights?" Pilot asked. Pilot gave the others a handful of jellybean beetles that he grabbed from the piñata. The jellybeans glowed in the dark room like a fire in the wilderness night but yet gave enough light to fill the darkness that circulated in the mysterious laboratory.

"The lights are beside you!" Lemon answered. Pilot flipped the switch, and Mr. Belvedere's workshop lit up like a kids eyes on Christmas morning. However, Lemon was nowhere to be found when the lights came on, and O'bey became sick to his stomach.

"Lemon..." he cried, "Where are thou, dude?" He cried a river onto Pilot's shoulder at the disappearance of Lemon. O'bey was very upset and could not concentrate.

"We'll find her." Pilot assured to his pal O'bey. Obey shook is head and wiped the tears from his cheek.

"You think so?" O'bey wandered. But before Pilot could respond, the children were distracted by the colors that illuminated the room like white teeth at the dentist. Every rotten candy from their journey stood before them, and more was being created by the second. Lemon wasn't missing but stood with her father and Sasha in the center of the room. The Princess played Pilot and the others since the Graham Cracker Pyramids and didn't care at all.

"Still in love O'bey?" Gully asked. O'bey was sad and didn't believe Lemon could do such a thing. He was embarrassed and hid his face. anymore.

"Hello, Pilot Blue," Mr. Belvedere said in a slithery voice, "What a pleasure to see you." Mr. Belvedere and his creations laughed that Pilot and the others became trapped with nowhere to go.

I have a surprise for you!" Mr. Belvedere gruesomely laughed. It was Pancho Vanilla. Mr. Belvedere baked Pancho bigger, stronger, and much angrier than before. He had a dispute to settle with Pilot.

"Where's my slingshot?" Pancho asked. He was mad that Pilot took his slingshot and turned him into vanilla extract.

"You'll have to ask O'bey." Pilot answered. O'bey shot a jaw-breaker at Pancho Vanilla with the slingshot causing him to fall to the ground. Pilot and the others scattered and a confrontation ensued between Lollyfudge's heroes and the rotten candy.

"I have you now!" Mr. Belvedere proclaimed. He laughed uncontrollably as the gumballs moved closer to the children. They were still trapped in the middle of the room and needed to act fast.

By a mere stroke of luck, the Licorice Indians and Bubblegum Soldiers burst into Mr. Belvedere's workshop, and once again saved the children. With all their might, the sweet candies fought the rotten ones as Pilot slipped away to get the rocket.

"Give me that rocket? Pilot demanded. The Rocket sat on a shelf behind Mr. Belvedere and Pilot needed to go through him to get it. Only one could have the rocket, and they both wanted it.

"Here it is my boy!" Mr. Belvedere chuckled. He raised his hands high and shot fireballs and jaw-breakers at Pilot, but Pilot rolled away and dodged them by an inch.

"You'll have to do better than that!" Pilot yelled as he fired and arrow at Mr. Belvedere from behind a crushed candy, however, Mr. Belvedere moved, and the arrow hit the rocket.

"Is that all you have, boy?" Mr. Belvedere asked. He laughed and called Creole Snake and Gumball Jack to his side. Pilot was again in trouble and needed help.

The rocket began to ignite and pull everything towards it, causing Mr. Belvedere's workshop to tremble. Candies fell from everywhere, and Pilot and Mr. Belvedere became trapped under a pile of rotten candy. O'bey looked for Lemon, and Gully ran to dig Pilot from under the pile of monsters.

"You lose, Pilot." Sasha meowed. Sasha grabbed the rocket and headed for the exit, but before she could leave, Rip showed up and snatched the rocket from her.

"I hate dogs!" Sasha meowed. She began to chase Rip everywhere in Mr. Belvedere's Rocket Candy Shop trying the get the rocket back.

"Give me that, you dumb dog!" She

meowed. Rip barked and kept running from her. It was a real "dog and cat" fight between those two and nobody was winning. Sasha became angry and went to enlist the help of her master, Mr. Belvedere.

In another part of the dark laboratory, Gully continued to dig Pilot from underneath the fallen candies.

"You're almost free!" Gully said. She pulled Pilot from the pile of candy and helped him to stand.

"We should leave!" Pilot encouraged. He called Rip, and they all headed for Sasha's cat hole. However, Rip slipped on a gumball, and the rocket flew in the air.

"I'll get the rocket!" Pilot said, "Go home!" O'bey and Gully went through the cat hole and ran to the house. Pilot stayed behind to get the rocket and finish the job.

The rotten candies were putting themselves together, and Pilot grabbed the rocket from the floor. He ran towards the cat hole with the rocket in his hands but was stopped by Mr. Belvedere at the last second.

"Were you going to leave without saying goodbye?" Mr. Belvedere asked. Mr. Belvedere wanted the rocket and held onto Pilot's leg tightly.

"Goodbye, Mr. Belvedere!" Pilot answered with a smirk on his face. At that moment, Rip bit Mr. Belvedere's leg and Pilot left the candy shop with the rocket.

Home at last

Pilot sat alone in the backyard looking at the candy moons. It was late, and Mrs. Blue came to take Pilot upstairs.

"Time for bed." Mrs. Blue said. "I wouldn't want the rotten candy to get you!" She walked Pilot upstairs and tucked him next to the others. There laid the three in total silence after exhaustion from their long journey to Mr. Belvederes Rocket Candy Shop.

"All that hard work for nothing!" Gully whispered. Gully was upset that she and the others didn't get the rocket and fussed about it.

"I wouldn't say that." Pilot answered with a smile. He had the rocket under his blanket and showed it to the two. The three closed their eyes and dreamt of the Rocket, and the next adventure with their Captain, Pilot Blue.

To be continued

ıbout the Author

native of Columbus, Mississippi nd a 2006 graduate of the 'niversity of Southen Mississippi, obert Harris Jr is the author of Ir. Belvedere's Rocket Candy hop; his very first novel . Robert as served honorably as an officer ı the United States Army, and :tended Southern University Law enter where he sharpened his riting skills and became ıterested in fictional writing.

oday, Robert has dedicated himself to raising his daughter maya and writing; as it was one of his mother's last 'ishes. Robert plans to expand his writing portfolio and is urrently working on the novels Mr. Belvedere's Candy arnival Circus and Mr. Belverdere Rocket Candy Shop 2.

Lollyfudge

Lightning Source UK Ltd.
Milton Keynes UK
UKHW012352270519
343433UK00001B/14/P

9 780991 315505